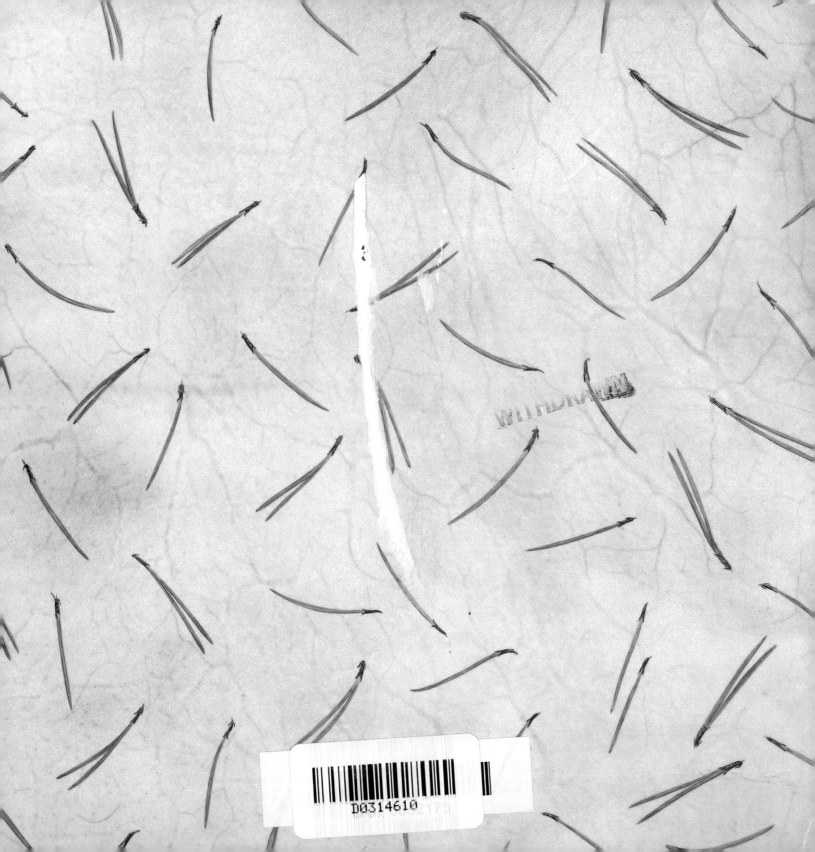

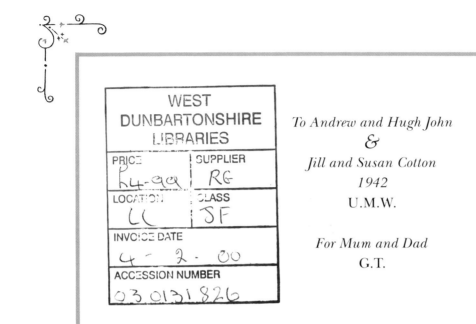
To Andrew and Hugh John
&
Jill and Susan Cotton
1942
U.M.W.

For Mum and Dad
G.T.

First published 1990 by Julia MacRae Books

This paperback edition published 1999
by Walker Books Ltd, 87 Vauxhall Walk
London SE11 5HJ

2 4 6 8 10 9 7 5 3

Text © 1943, 1990 Ursula Moray Williams
Illustrations © 1990 Gillian Tyler

Printed in Hong Kong

British Library Cataloguing in Publication Data
A catalogue record for this book is
available from the British Library.

ISBN 0-7445-7255-X

THE GOOD LITTLE
CHRISTMAS
TREE

Written by
Ursula Moray Williams

Illustrated by
Gillian Tyler

WALKER BOOKS
AND SUBSIDIARIES
LONDON • BOSTON • SYDNEY

One snowy Christmas Eve a peasant father walked home through the forest carrying a little Christmas Tree for his children.

It was neither a very tall nor a very fine tree; while the peasant, being a poor man, had no money to deck it about with gold and silver tinsel, dolls, kites, toys, and all the rest, but he did not worry overmuch about it. He knew his wife would discover something in the chest to make the little tree look splendid, and his children, who had never had such a thing in the house before, would be very well pleased.

When he reached home, having tied up the little Christmas Tree in a sack, he bundled it into a corner of the kitchen behind the stove, and nothing that his boy and girl could say or do could persuade him to say a word about it.

They danced about his legs, pointing, peering, and asking a thousand curious questions, while the father only shook his head; but if they approached too close to the stove to have a better look at the mysterious bundle he  shouted out, "Take care! Take care! There is a wolf in the sack!" till they ran to hide themselves behind their mother with little shrieks of terror and excitement.

Presently they grew tired of teasing and went to bed; and when the father and mother were sure that both slept soundly they took the Christmas Tree out of the corner, and set it in a pot, where the mother hung among its branches a number of little brown cookies that she had baked, tied with scarlet thread out of the chest.

The little tree looked very proud and fine, and at first the peasant and his wife admired it with all their hearts, but little by little doubt crept in, for like all parents they wished the best for their little children, and in five minutes they were sighing and shaking their heads like two pine trees on a hill as they said to each other,

"What a pity we have not the smallest silver star nor thread of tinsel to make the branches glitter!"

"How fine a few bright candles would look among the bushy needles! How the children's eyes would sparkle to watch them flicker!"

"How dingy the branches seem! So green and bare! If we had but a few small toys and gifts for our little ones, how they would clap their hands and jump for joy!"

"However, they are good, unselfish children," the parents agreed, preparing to go to bed; "they will think the tree very pretty as it is, and make the best of it."

So off they went, sighing a little, and leaving the little Christmas Tree alone on the kitchen floor.

The tree sighed, too, when the peasant and his wife were gone to bed, for they were an honest pair, and he liked their kind and simple hearts. The children, too, were well brought-up and cheerful, deserving the best that could come to them. If he could have crowded his humble branches with stars, diamonds, toys, bright ornaments, and playthings, the little Christmas Tree would have done so in a moment to please so worthy a family, and he stood

for a long while thinking deeply, with the cookies in their scarlet threads dangling from his branches like so many little brown mice.

All at once the little tree quivered. One by one he gently pulled his roots out of the pot. He moved so carefully that not a speck of earth fell upon the clean kitchen floor as he moved across to the door and peeped outside.

The snow lay white and deep all around. The pine trees drooped with it, but the world was well awake.

Far up in the Heavenly Meadows the baby Angels were preparing for a party.

There were wolves prowling in the forest and a pedlar, resting for the night, burned a fire to keep them away.

Mass was being sung in the far-off church, while by the

light of the moon gnomes and goblins were digging for diamonds under the snow.

Down by the stream a poor boy fished through a hole in the ice, hoping to get something for his supper, and Old Father Christmas, whom the peasants sometimes call St Nicholas, came walking through the forest with a sack over his shoulder.

The little Christmas Tree closed the door quietly behind him, running out into the snow with the cookies on his branches bobbing up and down like little brown mice as he hurried along.

He ran into a clearing where the gnomes and goblins were digging for diamonds. So busy were they that scarcely one looked up to notice him.

"What will you take for a few of your diamonds?" the little Christmas Tree asked the nearest goblins.

"Ten green needles! Ten green needles!" said the goblins, who used Christmas-tree needles for threading their necklaces of precious stones.

But when the little Christmas Tree had handed over his needles and had received three diamonds in exchange, the goblins suddenly caught sight of the cookies hanging on his branches, and called out:

"Ten green needles and a round brown cookie!"

Now the little Christmas Tree did not intend to part with any of the cookies the peasant mother had made for her children, but in order to pacify the goblins he had to give them first another ten, and then a further dozen, of his green needles, after which he left them and trotted on  his way, with the diamonds sparkling among his branches and the cookies bobbing up and down like little brown mice.

When he had left the goblins far behind he came on a circle of scarlet toadstools, so bright and splendid with their red tops all spotted with white, that he knew it would delight the children to see a few peeping from among his needles.

But he had hardly helped himself to a handful before he heard a terrible baying, which came nearer and nearer and nearer. Surrounding him was a ring of wolves, their tongues hanging out, their eyes green and hungry.

"Don't you know better than to pick scarlet toadstools?" they asked the little Christmas Tree. "Don't you know that every time you pluck one a bell rings in the Wolves' Den?"

"What will you take for your red toadstools?" the little Christmas Tree asked, trembling with fear.

"Twenty green needles! Twenty green needles!" said the wolves, who used Christmas-tree needles for picking thorns out of their paws. But when the little tree had plucked out the needles they noticed the cookies hanging among his branches, and growled out,

"Twenty green needles and two brown cookies!"

Now the little Christmas Tree did not intend to let the wolves have any of the cookies the peasant mother had baked for her children, so he made one bound out of the circle, shaking a shower of sharp needles into the wolves' faces, sending them howling into the forest. He then went on his way, with the toadstools gleaming, the diamonds glittering, and the cookies bobbing about like little brown mice.

Now he came to a stream out of which all movement seemed frozen. But underneath the ice the fish still swam in the current, and here, beside a bridge hung with silver icicles, a poor boy had made a hole in the ice and was fishing for his supper.

The Christmas Tree was about to cross the bridge when he noticed the icicles, and thought how pretty a few would look hanging from the tips of his boughs like spears.

"What will you take for a few of those icicles?" he asked the fisher-boy.

"They are not mine to sell," the poor boy replied. "God made the icicles; I suppose He means us to take what we please. But pray tread carefully, or you will frighten away my little fishes."

The little Christmas Tree was so pleased with the boy's courtesy that when he had broken away a few beautiful icicles he handed some of his own green needles to the fisher-boy to make new hooks.

The boy thanked him gratefully, but his eyes strayed so wistfully towards the cookies hanging among the branches that the little tree felt much perplexed.

He could not part with any of the cookies the peasant mother had made for her children, but he said, "If you wish, you may take one bite out of my largest cookie, for I feel sure that is what any mother would wish!"

The boy eagerly did as he was told, and immediately felt as if he had risen from a banquet of roast goose, turkey, venison, plum-pudding, mince-pies, jellies, and dessert, while the little Christmas Tree hurried on his way, with the icicles sparkling, the toadstools gleaming, the diamonds glittering, and the cookies bobbing about like little brown mice.

Soon he met a procession of people who were wending their way through the forest to church.

All were carrying candles which they lit as they passed through the door, where already a great number of people were singing and praising God.

The little Christmas Tree crept in behind them to listen. In the nave stood trees a great deal taller than he, their branches ablaze with coloured candles that flickered

as if they too were singing anthems.

The little tree dared not ask for a candle, so he stood close by the door, listening and watching for quite a long while.

Presently an old man and a young girl came into the church. The girl took coloured candles out of her basket, lighted them, and tied them on to the branches of the little Christmas Tree.

"There! That will please the good angels and amuse some poor child on Christmas morning," said the girl.

But the old man grumbled, "Look at all those cookies hanging on the branches! They will do no good there! They will go bad! The mice will eat them during the night! They ought to be cut off and given to the poor!"

The little Christmas Tree trembled so much at the old man's words that quite a shower of green needles fell on the floor round the young girl's feet, and, as she and the old man walked up the church to join the singing, the little tree quickly slipped through the door and out into the forest, with the candles flickering, the icicles sparkling, the toadstools gleaming, the diamonds glittering, and the cookies bobbing about like little brown mice.

Soon he had left the church far behind.

Deep in the forest he came upon a pedlar sitting by his dying fire. Beside him all his wares were spread out on the snow – puppets, boats, knives, ribbons, shawls, a fine wooden horse, and a dainty little pair of red slippers.

"What will you take for that wooden horse, and that dainty pair of slippers?" asked the little Christmas Tree.

"Enough wood to make my fire blaze. I am freezing to death!" replied the pedlar.

The little Christmas Tree began to throw handfuls of his green needles into the fire, but they only smouldered. Then he broke off some of his lower twigs. They crackled a little and went out. Then he broke off his best branch, and the fire burst into a bright blaze.

The pedlar gave the wooden horse to the little Christmas Tree, but when he saw the cookies hanging on

the branches a greedy look came into his eyes and he said, "If you want the slippers, too, you must give me three of those round brown cookies!"

But the little Christmas Tree did not intend to part with any of the cookies the peasant mother had made for her children.

"Oh no!" said he, "that was not our bargain at all! But I will give you another branch to keep your fire alight, and you shall give me the red slippers."

The pedlar grumbled and complained, but before he could change his mind the little Christmas Tree threw another branch on the fire, picked up the slippers, and ran away with them into the forest, with the wooden horse prancing, the candles flickering, the icicles sparkling, the toadstools gleaming, the diamonds glittering, and the cookies bobbing about like little brown mice.

He ran right into the Heavenly Meadows where the baby Angels were holding their party.

They were so pleased to see him they clustered round him, caressing him with their soft little wings. Their pink toes peeped out from under their white nightgowns, and they clapped their little pink hands together in joy and delight.

When they had danced around him nearly a hundred times they began to tie their brightest stars to his boughs. No wonder that the little Christmas Tree glowed with pleasure and gratitude!

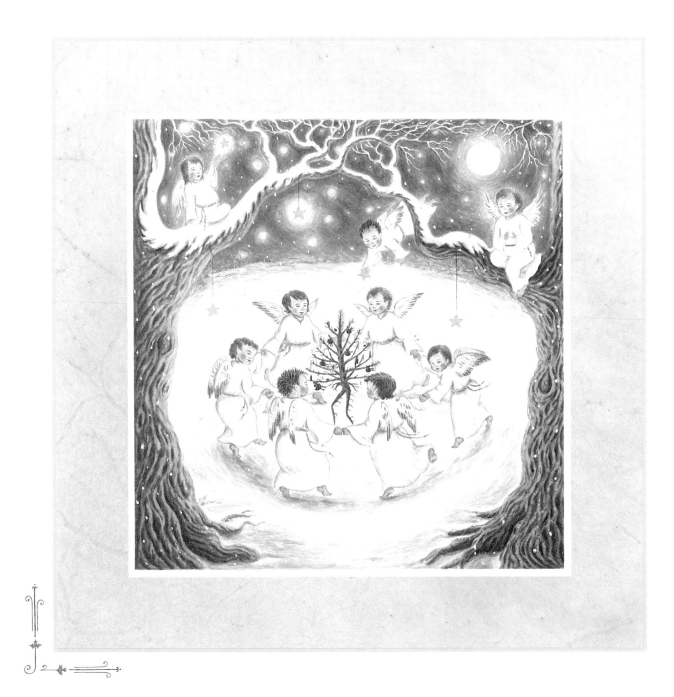

He had very few needles left on his branches, but he offered them all as playthings to the baby Angels.

But when they grew tired of playing with the pretty green needles they began to beg for the cookies, stretching out their little hands for them and clamouring, as children will.

Now the little Christmas Tree did not intend to part with any of the cookies the peasant mother had made for her children, but the baby Angels had been so kind to him, and their rosy faces were so beseeching, that he had not the heart to refuse them, so at last he said: "Each of you may take a tiny bite out of just one cookie, for I feel sure that is what any mother would wish!"

But when the baby Angels had had one bite they all wanted another, and to escape them the little Christmas Tree had to take to his heels and run until he had left the

Heavenly Meadows far behind, with the stars shining, the slippers flapping, the wooden horse prancing, the candles flickering, the icicles sparkling, the toadstools gleaming, the diamonds glittering, and the cookies bobbing about like little brown mice.

He ran till the forest was dark again, and there he found a pool, so deep and so clear that the ice had not covered it at all.

"I will have just one drink of cool water," said the little Christmas Tree, "then I must be going home."

But when he bent over the pool and saw his reflection

in the moonlight he was so overcome by his miserable appearance that he shrank back into the snow as if he wished to hide himself completely. Gone were his bushy needles with their pale green tips, the jaunty fingers outstretched from each sturdy bough. Some of the boughs themselves were gone, leaving jagged, miserable stumps behind. It was as if the stars, the slippers, the horse, the candles, the icicles, the toadstools, and the diamonds hung on the arms of some ragged scarecrow!

He was ashamed to go home!

While the little Christmas Tree lay almost dying of shame in the snow, someone came tramping through the forest, bringing with him joy and gladness.

St Nicholas is the children's saint. Sometimes they call him Old Father Christmas, and sometimes Santa Claus, and they credit him with all kinds of strange tricks and ways. They say he drives reindeer across the starry skies, halting them on snowy roofs to dive down chimneys with loads of gifts for stockings, sabots, and shoes. They leave presents for him, milk and cake and wine, and hay in the shoes for his reindeer. They know very little about him, but they say a great deal, and every little child loves him dearly.

The peasant's children were awake and peeping through the window, as children will on Christmas night.

"Look! Look what is coming through the forest! Look at the wolves! Look at the gnomes and goblins! Look at the sweet little Angels in their white nightgowns! Look at the people singing, and the poor boy carrying his basket of fish! Look at the pedlarman! and *look!* … there is Old Father Christmas, and he is bringing us a little Christmas Tree all covered with…Oh! quick! quick!get back into bed and pull the bedclothes over our heads as quick as we can, or we shall never get anything at all."

MORE WALKER PAPERBACKS
For You to Enjoy

THE CHRISTMAS KITTEN
by Vivian French / Chris Fisher

It's the day before Christmas. Out in the snow, the little black kitten is cold and hungry and lonely.
Nobody seems to want him. But, at last, he stumbles on Father Christmas,
who knows just where the little kitten belongs!

0-7445-7214-2   £4.99

MIMI'S CHRISTMAS
by Martin Waddell / Leo Hartas

Christmas is coming and Mimi's mouse brothers and sisters all write their notes to Santa Mouse.
Little Hugo asks for a drum. But on Christmas Eve he can't sleep and he's afraid Santa Mouse
won't come. Luckily, Mimi is on hand to reassure him in this delightful tale
by the author of *Can't You Sleep, Little Bear?*

0-7445-7213-4   £4.99

RUBY THE CHRISTMAS DONKEY
by Mirabel Cecil / Christina Gascoigne

Poor Ruby is growing old and can't keep herself warm in the winter.
So the other animals make her a special gift – a colourful Christmas coat –
in this heartwarming seasonal tale.

"Christina Gascoigne's illustrations are a real delight." *The Sunday Telegraph*

0-7445-6385-2   £4.99

Walker Paperbacks are available from most booksellers, or by post from B.B.C.S., P.O. Box 941, Hull, North Humberside HU1 3YQ
24 hour telephone credit card line 01482 224626
To order, send: Title, author, ISBN number and price for each book ordered, your full name and address,
cheque or postal order payable to BBCS for the total amount and allow the following for postage and packing:
UK and BFPO: £1.00 for the first book, and 50p for each additional book to a maximum of £3.50.
Overseas and Eire: £2.00 for the first book, £1.00 for the second and 50p for each additional book.
Prices and availability are subject to change without notice.